This book
belongs to

_____

# Much More Munsch!

## A Robert Munsch Collection

Illustrated by

**Michael Martchenko**

and

**Alan and Lea Daniel**

**Scholastic Canada Ltd.**
New York  Toronto  London  Auckland  Sydney
Mexico City  New Delhi  Hong Kong  Buenos Aires

Scholastic Canada Ltd.
604 King Street West, Toronto, Ontario M5V 1E1, Canada

Scholastic Inc.
557 Broadway, New York, NY 10012, USA

Scholastic Australia Pty Limited
PO Box 579, Gosford, NSW 2250, Australia

Scholastic New Zealand Limited
Private Bag 94407, Greenmount, Auckland, New Zealand

Scholastic Children's Books
Euston House, 24 Eversholt Street, London NW1 1DB, UK


**Library and Archives Canada Cataloguing in Publication**
Munsch, Robert N., 1945-
    Much more Munsch : a Robert Munsch collection / illustrations
by Michael Martchenko, Alan Daniel and Lea Daniel.

Includes never-published-before poems.
Complete contents:  We share everything! — Aaron's hair — Up, up,
    down — Makeup mess — Playhouse.
ISBN 978-0-439-93571-5

    I. Martchenko, Michael  II. Daniel, Alan, 1939-  III. Daniel, Lea
IV. Title.

PS8576.U575M83 2007          C813'.54          C2007-902214-6

ISBN-13 978-0-439-93571-5
ISBN-10 0-439-93571-7

LEGO ® is a trademark of The LEGO Group.

6 5 4 3 2          Printed in Singapore          07 08 09 10 11

# Contents

*To Amanda McCusker
and Jeremiah Williams
Pontiac, Michigan*

*— R.M.*

# We Share
# EVERYTHING!

by **Robert Munsch**

illustrated by **Michael Martchenko**

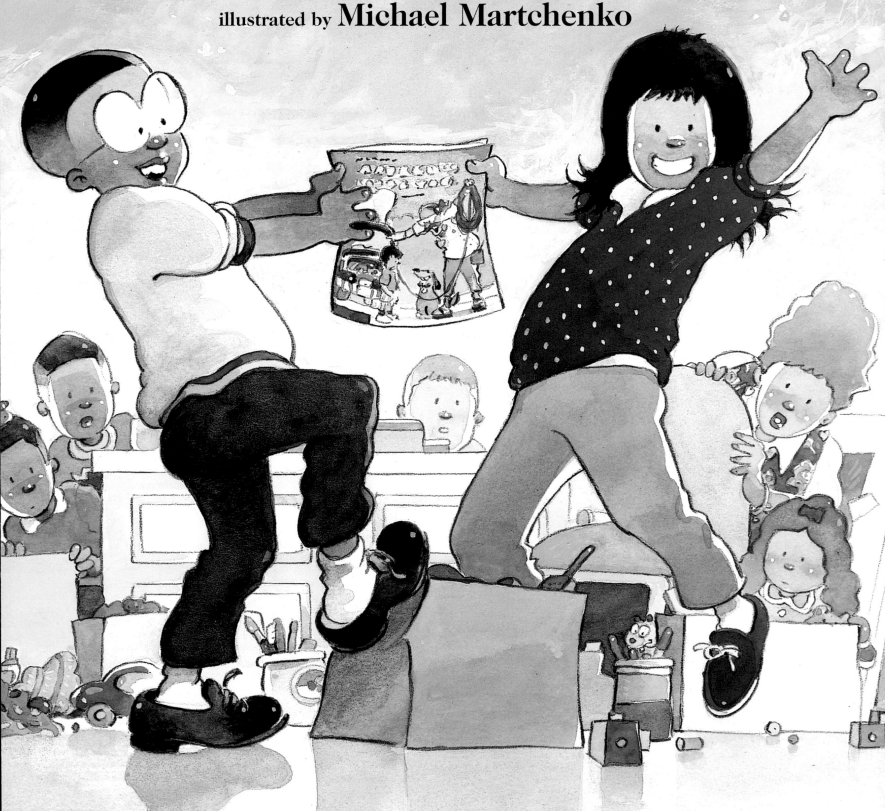

$O$n their very first day of school,

when they didn't know what to do,

Amanda and Jeremiah walked into the kindergarten classroom and Amanda picked up a book.

Jeremiah came over to her and said, "Give me that book."

Amanda said, "No, I won't give you this book. I'm looking at this book."

So Jeremiah tried what worked with his little brother. He said, "If you don't give me that book, I am going to yell and scream."

"Too bad!" said Amanda.

So Jeremiah opened his mouth really wide and screamed:

"AAAAAAAAHHHHH!"

Amanda stuck the book in his mouth:

*BLUMPH!*

Jeremiah said, "GAWCK!"

The teacher came running over
and said,
  "Now, LOOK!
This is kindergarten.
In kindergarten we share.
We share *everything*."
  "Okay, okay, okay, okay, okay,"
said Amanda and Jeremiah.

Jeremiah started to build a tower with blocks.

Amanda came over and said, "Give me those blocks."

"I won't give you the blocks," said Jeremiah. "I'm building a tower."

So Amanda tried what worked with her older brother. She said, "If you don't give me those blocks, I am going to kick them down!"

"Too bad," said Jeremiah.

So Amanda kicked the blocks:

CRASH!

Blocks went all over the floor.
Amanda yelled: Ouch!

Owww!

Ouch!

Owww!

Ouch!

Ouch!

Owww!

The teacher came running over
and said,
    "Now, LOOK!
    This is kindergarten.
    In kindergarten we share.
    We share *everything.*"
    "Okay, okay, okay, okay, okay,"
said Amanda and Jeremiah.

Then Jeremiah and Amanda
went to play with the paint.

"I'm first," said Jeremiah.

"No! I'm first," said Amanda.

"If you don't let me go first,"
said Jeremiah, "I am going to yell
and scream."

"Too bad," said Amanda.

So Jeremiah and Amanda were both first,
and paint went flying all over the room.

Jeremiah yelled as loud as he could:

## "AAAAAAHHHHHH!"

The teacher and all the kids
came running over and said,
"Now, LOOK!
This is kindergarten.
In kindergarten we share.
We share *everything*."

So Jeremiah looked at Amanda and said, "Okay, Amanda, we are supposed to share. What are we going to share?"

"I don't know," said Amanda. "Let's share . . . let's share . . . let's share our shoes."

"Good idea!" said Jeremiah.

So they shared their shoes and Jeremiah said, "Look at this. Pink shoes, and they fit just right. My mom never gets me pink shoes. This is great! Let's share . . . Let's share . . . Let's share our shirts."

So they shared their shirts, and Jeremiah said, "Look at this. A pink shirt. No other boy in kindergarten has a pink shirt."

"Yes," said Amanda. "This is fun. Let's share . . . Let's share . . . Let's share our pants."

So they shared their pants.

"Wow!" said Jeremiah. "Pink pants!"

The teacher came back and said, "Oh, Jeremiah and Amanda. You're sharing, and you're learning how to act in kindergarten, and you're being very grown-up, and Jeremiah, I really like your . . . PINK PANTS! Jeremiah, where did you get those pink pants?"

"Oh," said Jeremiah, "It's okay. Amanda and I shared our clothes."

The teacher yelled, "What have you done? Who said you could share your clothes?"

And all the kids said:
"Now, LOOK!
This is kindergarten.
In kindergarten
we share . . . "

"We share EVERYTHING!"

# About
# We Share Everything

In 1998, a kindergarten in Pontiac, Michigan, wrote me a neat letter and I decided to go visit. This kindergarten had an interesting problem named Jeremiah. Jeremiah's shoes were too big for his feet, and Jeremiah had a really simple solution for this. He started every day at kindergarten by switching shoes with someone else. He did not tell the other person that he was switching shoes. Jeremiah just walked around the room till he found some shoes to switch with. This caused *lots* of fights about shoes, but it gave me the idea for a story about a kid who switched shoes, and this quickly changed to a story about a kid who switched *everything*.

Amanda got to be in the story because I was staying with her family while I visited the school. The teacher had a lottery to see who I would stay with, and Amanda won the lottery. She was really happy to be in the book, but she wants to make it clear that she and Jeremiah never *really* switched their clothes. They only switched shoes — and that was all Jeremiah's idea.

— R.M.

*This book is dedicated to Aaron Riches, whose pre-school teacher I was in 1980, and to Miriam and Leah Riches, the sisters; to Bill and Judy Riches, the mommy and daddy; to downtown Guelph, Ontario, and its fountain with the statue. And to the Guelph Police, who always give me parking tickets and valiantly try to defend the downtown statue from the children of Guelph.*

*—R.M.*

# Aaron's Hair

BY ROBERT MUNSCH

ILLUSTRATED BY

ALAN & LEA DANIEL

Aaron wanted to look just like his daddy.
So he let his hair get long . . . only then he
started to have problems.

If he combed his hair up, his hair flipped down.

If he combed his hair down, his hair flipped up.

If he combed his hair over, his hair flipped under.

If he combed his hair under, his hair flipped over.

One day, while Aaron was combing his hair, he got so mad that he yelled,

"HAIR! I HATE YOU!"

38

39

That hurt the hair's feelings.
It jumped off Aaron's head and
ran out of the bathroom.

When Aaron came downstairs,
his mother said, "Aaron, you're
bald! What happened?"
"My hair ran away," said Aaron.
"I got mad at it, and it ran away."

"This is terrible!" said his mother.
"Go catch it."

So Aaron ran out the door, and his mother went to pick up the baby. She noticed that the baby had a lot of hair.

"Aaron!" she yelled.
"I found your hair!"

But when Aaron ran back inside, the hair jumped
over his head and ran out the door and down the street.

So Aaron chased it down the street.
After a while, he came to a lady who
was yelling and screaming,

"HELP! HELP!
HELP! HELP!"

"What's the matter?"
asked Aaron.

46

"Look at my tummy," said the lady. "This hair came running down the street and now it is growing on my tummy!"

"It does look a little strange," said Aaron.

"MAKE IT GO AWAY!" said the lady.

"Just tell it to get off," said Aaron. "Tell it you don't like it."

The lady yelled,

"HAIR! I HATE YOU!"

The hair jumped off the lady and ran down the street, and Aaron ran after it.

Next Aaron came to a man who was running around in circles yelling,

"HELP! HELP! HELP! HELP!"

"What's the matter?" asked Aaron.

49

"Look at me!" said the man. "This hair came running down the street, and now it is growing on my behind!"

"It does look a little strange," said Aaron.

"MAKE IT GO AWAY!"
yelled the man.

"Just tell it to get off," said Aaron.
"Tell it you don't like it."

The man yelled,

# "HAIR! I HATE YOU!"

The hair jumped off the man
and ran down the street, and
Aaron ran after it.

Aaron chased it all the way to the middle of downtown, where there was an enormous traffic jam. A policeman was screaming,

"HELP! HELP! HELP! HELP!"

Aaron went to the policeman and said, "That's my hair."

"Your hair!" said the policeman. "This hair came running down the street, ran up my back, and started growing on my face. I can't see a thing. I am supposed to be directing traffic and **EVERYTHING** is all jammed up!"

52

53

"Right," said Aaron.
"What a mess! Ten cars,
nine motorcycles,
eight trucks,
seven buses,
six baby carriages,
five skateboards,
four bicycles,
three ambulances,
two fire trucks,
and one train."

55

"And my face!" said the policeman. "This hair is growing on my face!"

"It does look a little strange," said Aaron.

"MAKE IT GO AWAY," yelled the policeman.

"Just tell it to get off," said Aaron. "Tell it you don't like it."

So the policeman yelled,

"HAIR! I HATE YOU!"

The hair jumped off the policeman's face and ran into the pile of cars.

"Oh, no!" said Aaron. "Now I'll never find it."

Just then the police chief came up and said,
"What is going on? Everything is all jammed up —
and who put that hair on the statue?"

"Statue?" said Aaron.

"The statue in the fountain," said the police chief.
"The one you kids always mess around with!
Get that hair off the statue!"

So Aaron climbed up the statue and almost caught the hair, but it ran away and Aaron chased it all the way home.

And then he couldn't find it at all.

60

At dinner Aaron said, "I'm bald forever.
I wish my hair would come back.

# I LIKE MY HAIR."

And the hair jumped off the father's head onto
the table, ran over the mashed potatoes, peas,
and chicken, and climbed back onto Aaron's head.
  "Fantastic," said Aaron. "Now if I can
just grow a beard, I will look like Daddy."

"No problem,"
said the hair.

64

# About Aaron's Hair

In 1976 I was Aaron's nursery school teacher. Aaron always had messy hair that was very hard to comb. This was sort of strange, because Aaron sometimes came to nursery school wearing a suit and a tie. He was the *only* kid I ever had in nursery school that came in a suit and tie. Lots of kids in nursery school have messy hair, but they do not have messy hair while they wear a suit and tie. So I made up a hair story for Aaron where his hair ran away.

Fifteen years later I tracked down Aaron. He was living in Toronto and was the leader of a rock band. His hair was out-of-sight-super-messy! Much more messy than when he was a little kid! I said "Aaron, would you mind if I made the messy hair story into a book?"

"No," said Aaron. "Would you mind if my messy-haired band plays for the book launch?"

So the book launch for the messy hair story had a messy-haired band playing loud music with a messy-haired band leader.

— R.M.

To Anna James,
Guelph, Ontario
— R.M.

by **Robert Munsch**

illustrated by **Michael Martchenko**

# Up, Up, Down

One day Anna, who liked to climb, walked into the kitchen and started to climb up the refrigerator.

She went

up, up, up, up, up, up . . . Falllll down.

And landed right on her head.

"OW OUCH! OW OUCH! OW OUCH! OW OUCH!

Anna's mother saw her and said,
"Be careful! Don't climb!"

But Anna didn't listen. She went to
her bedroom and tried to climb up
her dresser.
She went

up, up, up, up, up, up . . . Falllll down.

And landed right on her tummy.

"OW OUCH! OW OUCH! OW OW OUCH!"

Her father found her on the floor and
said, "Be careful! Don't climb."
So Anna decided to go outside where it
was okay to climb, and the biggest thing
she could find to climb was . . .

The Tree.

Anna went

up, up, up, up, up, up . . . Fallllll down.

And landed right on her bottom.

"OW OUCH! OW OUCH! OW OUCH! OW OUCH!

78

But the next time she was very careful.
She went

up . . .
up, up, up,
up, up, up, up, up,

all the way to the top of the tree.

80

And then Anna yelled,
"I'm the king of the castle,
Mommy's a dirty rascal!"

83

Anna's mother came out of the house
and looked all around. She said,
  "Anna? Anna? Anna?

# ANNA!
# Get out of that tree!"

And Anna said, "No, no, no, no, no!"

So her mother tried to climb the tree.
She went

up, up, up, up, up, up . . . Fallllll down.

And landed right on her head.

"OW OUCH! OW OUCH! OW OUCH! OW OUCH!

And then Anna yelled, "I'm the king of the castle, Daddy's a dirty rascal."

Anna's father came out of the house and looked all around.

He said, "Anna? Anna? Anna?

# ANNA!
# Get out of that tree!"

And Anna said, "No, no, no, no, no!"

So her father tried to climb the tree.
He went

up, up, up, up, up, up . . . Falllll down.

And landed right on his bottom.

"OW OUCH! OW OUCH! OW OUCH! OW OUCH!

Anna leaned over the side of the tree. She looked at her mother and she looked at her father. Her mother was holding her head and yelling,

## "WAHHHHH!"

And her father was holding his bottom and yelling,

"OW OUCH! OW OUCH! OUCH! OW OUCH!

Then Anna climbed

down, down, down, down, down, down,

all the way to the bottom of the tree.
She got her brother and sisters, and
they ran inside and got ten enormous
Band-Aids.

Anna walked over to her mother, took the paper off one Band-Aid:

# SCRITCH!

And wrapped it around her mother's head:

WRAP WRAP WRAP WRAP WRAP.

Then Anna walked over to her father, took the paper off the other Band-Aid:

# SCRITCH!

And wrapped it around her father's bottom:

WRAP WRAP WRAP WRAP WRAP.

Then Anna looked at her mother and
she looked at her father and she said,

"Be CAREFUL — don't CLIMB!"

# About Up, Up, Down

*Up, Up, Down* started in 1975, as a finger play that I used with children in daycare. I said: "UP-UP-UP-UP-UP-UP-FALL DOWN," while I raised my hands and then fell down. The kids imitated me and loved the game. It was a great hit with two-year-old kids.

I kept using it and quite slowly it turned into a story as I kept finding ways to use it with older kids. After about four years it settled into the version that is in the book. The last change was adding "I'm the King of the Castle" — but *I still did not have a kid for it.*

I thought of Anna James because she lived near us and was a lively, climby sort of kid. Much later, when the story finally became a book, Anna was on her college basketball team and really *was* going up and down a lot!

— R.M.

# Makeup Mess

by **Robert Munsch**

illustrated by
**Michael Martchenko**

Julie had saved up lots of money. She had saved up her birthday money, her Christmas money, and her paper route money, and she had robbed her little brother's piggy bank. All together, she had one hundred dollars.

Julie walked out the door holding
all that money and her mother said,
"Julie, where are you going?"

"I," said Julie, "am going to go buy
myself some MMMMMAKEUP!"

Julie's mother yelled, "Oh, no!"

Julie didn't pay any attention. She ran to the drugstore, put the money down, and said, "I want some red lipstick, blue lipstick, black lipstick, pink lipstick, yellow lipstick, purple lipstick . . . I want one of everything you've got."

The man gave Julie an enormous box of makeup. She picked it up, carried it home, and took it into the bathroom. Then she said, "Now I am going to make myself BEEEEEEAUTIFUL!"

So Julie took some purple stuff and stuck it on her eyes. She took some green stuff and put it on her cheeks. She took some black stuff and put it on her lips, and she coloured her hair purple. Then she put nineteen earrings in one ear and seventeen earrings in the other ear.

Julie looked in the mirror and said, "Wow, I am as pretty as a movie star!"

Julie ran downstairs and went into the kitchen. Her mother looked at her and yelled,

**"AAAAAHHHHHH!"**

Julie said, "What's the matter with my mother? She's acting very strange today."

Then Julie walked into the living room. Her father looked up and yelled,

**"AAAAAHHHHHH!"**

Julie said, "What's the matter with my father? He's acting very strange today."

Julie ran back upstairs, washed off all the makeup, and started over. This time she took some yellow stuff and stuck it on her eyes. She took some purple stuff and put it on her cheeks. She took some green stuff and put it on her lips, and she coloured her hair red.

Then she put nineteen earrings in one ear, seventeen earrings in the other ear, and two rings in her nose.

Julie looked in the mirror and said, "Wow, I'm as pretty as TWO movie stars!"

She walked downstairs and went into the living room. Her mother saw her and didn't say anything. She just fell right over.

Then Julie walked into the kitchen. Her father saw her and didn't say anything. He just fell right over.

Then someone knocked at the door: *BLAM, BLAM, BLAM, BLAM, BLAM.*

Julie opened the door. It was the mailman. He didn't say anything either. He just fell right over.

"Oh, dear," said Julie. "I must have made a terrible mistake with my makeup."

Julie ran upstairs and washed everything off. Then she looked in the mirror and said, "Oh, no! I spent one hundred dollars and all I have left is my regular face. This is terrible. Nobody will think that I'm pretty!"

Julie walked downstairs. Her mother got up off the floor, and her father got up off the floor, and the mailman got up off the floor, and they all said, "Now you're really learning how to use makeup! Now you're REALLY BEAUTIFUL!"

Julie said, "But, but, but . . . I don't have on any makeup at all!" Then she ran back up the stairs, looked in the mirror, and yelled, "LOOK AT ME! I'M BEAUTIFUL WITH NO MAKEUP!"

Then Julie leaned out the window and yelled, "WHO WANTS TO BUY SOME MAKEUP?"

All the girls in the neighbourhood came running and asked, "How much?"

"Three hundred dollars," said Julie.

So all the girls ran and got their birthday money and their New Year's money and their tooth fairy money, and they gave Julie the three hundred dollars.

Then they ran into Julie's bathroom and yelled, "Now I am going to make myself BEEEEEAUTIFUL!"

And Julie used some of the money to pay back her little brother, and she took the rest to the thrift store to buy lots of old clothes for . . .

DRESS-UP!

# About Makeup Mess

In November of 1984 I was supposed to be telling stories at the Northern Arts and Cultural Centre in Yellowknife, Northwest Territories. I did not make it to the show because I got stuck in a three-day blizzard on Victoria Island in the Arctic Ocean. When I finally got to Yellowknife, I did a quick replacement show for anyone who could come. I ended up with a strange audience that had lots of really little kids — and two teenage girls. I wanted to use one of the teenage girls in a story, but I did not have any good stories for teenage girls.  So I made up a makeup story because I figured that the girls would like one. They were both wearing lots of makeup. I left right after the show and I never got to talk to the girl in the makeup story. I even forgot her name.

Fifteen years later when I wanted to make the story into a book I decided to use my daughter Julie, who loved to do face painting and makeup when she was growing up. The last picture in the book, where Julie is doing dress-up, is from a photo. When Julie did dress-up, she did it really all the way!

— R.M.

*To Rene Jakubowski
and her family,
Endeavour, Saskatchewan
— R.M.*

by **Robert Munsch**

# Playhouse

illustrated by **Michael Martchenko**

One day, Rene went to her father and said, "Pleeeeeease make me a playhouse! Our farm is way out in the middle of the woods, and I have nobody to play with except my little brothers. I need a playhouse."

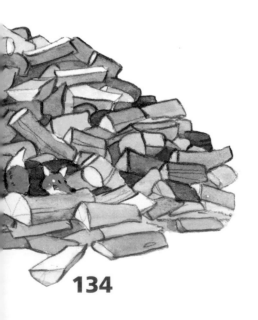

"Good idea," said Rene's father, and he made her a wonderful playhouse. It had real windows and a slide and a ladder and an upstairs and a downstairs. It was almost like a real house — but not quite.

The next day, Rene moved lots of stuff from her room into the new playhouse, and it was even more like a real house. Then she drew fish all over the walls of the playhouse, just like the ones on the wall of her real bedroom.

Rene was happy for a whole week.
Then she went to her mother and said,
"Is this a city playhouse or a farm playhouse?"
"Well, Rene," said her mother, "we live on
a farm, so this must be a farm playhouse."

"Good," said Rene. "If it's a farm playhouse, it needs a play barn."

"A play what?" said her mother.

"A play barn," said Rene.

"I never heard of a play barn," said Rene's mother, but she was such a nice mother that she built Rene a play barn. It took her two weeks.

Rene moved some hay and some chickens from the real barn into her play barn, and it was almost like a real barn — but not quite.

Then Rene went to her father and said, "I need a play cow."

"A play what?" said her father.

"A play cow," said Rene. "A farm playhouse needs a play barn, needs a play cow."

"I can't build a play cow," said Rene's father, "and the play barn is not big enough for a real cow."

"No problem," said Rene. "How about you give me a goat and paint it so it looks like a cow, and then I will have a play cow."

So Rene's father got her a goat and painted it so it looked like a cow. Rene put her play cow, which was really a goat, in the play barn, and she felt like she had a farm of her own — but not quite.

Then Rene went to her father and said, "My play farm is out in the middle of the woods just like our real farm, so it needs the tractor and the bulldozer and the tree snipper and the log chopper. Why don't you just park them by my playhouse, and then you will not have to make me anything new?"

So her father parked the tractor and the bulldozer and the tree snipper and the log chopper beside the playhouse, and Rene played quite nicely for a whole month.

Then Rene went to her mother and said, "A farm playhouse needs a play barn, needs a play cow, needs a play tractor, needs a play mommy and a play daddy."

"A play who and a play what?" said her mother.

"A play mommy and a play daddy," said Rene.

"No," said Rene's mother. "You already have a real mommy and a real daddy. You don't need a play mommy and a play daddy."

"The real ones are too bossy," said Rene.

"Ha!" said her mother. "I am not going to make you a play mommy and a play daddy."

So Rene cut out a cardboard play mommy and a cardboard play daddy and stuck them on the side of her playhouse, and while she was at it, she made two play brothers.

When Rene came in for dinner, there was a scarecrow sitting in her chair.

"What's that?" said Rene.

"That," said her mother, "is my Play Rene. She is always nice and never bossy. You can eat play food out in the playhouse with your play mommy and your play daddy."

Rene said, "Play Rene and I are going to go outside."

Then the real Rene took Play Rene and fed it to the play cow, which was really a goat. The goat ate all the clothes and all the straw, and soon Play Rene was completely gone.

Then Rene walked into the kitchen and gave her mother a kiss.

"Was that a real kiss or a play kiss?" said Rene's mother.

"That," said Rene, "was a real kiss, from a real bossy daughter for a real bossy mommy. Now can I have a real dinner with my real family?"

"No problem," said her mother. "I like real bossy kids better than play kids anyway."

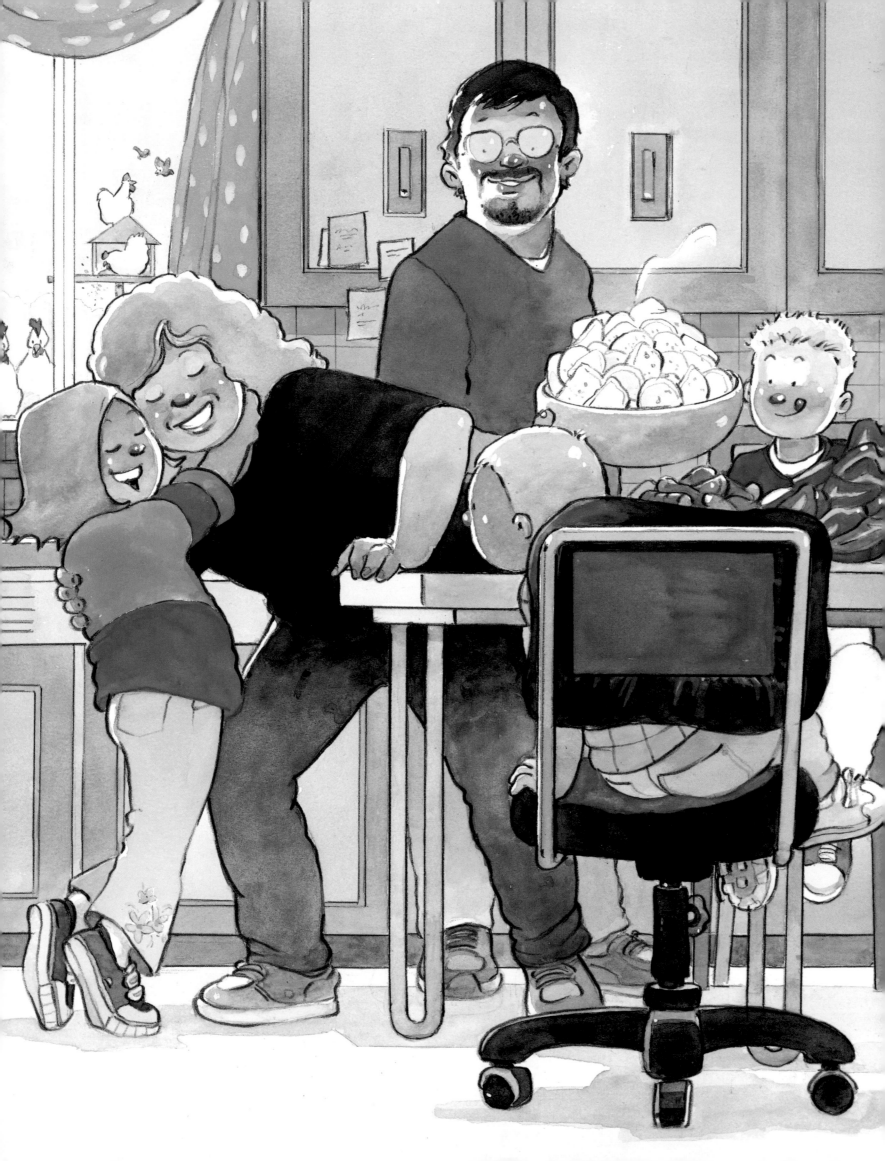

And everyone had a
real wonderful dinner.

# About PLAYHOUSE

In 1996 I received a package of letters from the grade two at Endeavour Elementary School in Endeavour, Saskatchewan. It was a small package since only five kids were in class that day. That was because it was -50 degrees outside and most of the kids had decided to stay home. One of the letters was from Rene Jakubowski, and it had a neat drawing of a playhouse on it. I liked the drawing so much that I made up a little playhouse story for Rene. In the story she keeps asking for strange things like a play barn and a play tractor. Rene liked the story and sent me a photo of her real playhouse.

WOW!

It was quite a playhouse — it had two stories and a balcony and a slide! I had thought that her drawing of a playhouse with two stories and a balcony and a slide was a drawing of a *pretend* playhouse, but it turned out that it was a drawing of her *real* playhouse.

In 1999 I decided to visit Rene's playhouse.

WOW!

Rene's farm had tractors and cultivators and tree snippers and tree snappergrabbers and lots of other stuff. *And* Rene's bedroom had fish painted on the walls. I decided then and there to make the playhouse story into a book. I took lots of pictures to give to Michael Martchenko, so all the stuff in the book is real except for the one pterodactyl that Michael hid in a flock of Canada geese. I had not taken pictures of any pterodactyls.

— R.M.

# Poems

# Caleb

Caleb likes Lego
And Lego likes him.
They play well together
With vigour and vim.
They cover the floor
And fill up the house
There's not even room
For a cat or a mouse.
His mother and father
Do sometimes complain
That Caleb likes Lego
And Lego's a pain.
But Caleb is happy
And Caleb is swell;
And if you like Caleb,
Like Lego as well.

*For Caleb Stratton,*
*Ballston Lake, New York.*
*"I invent crazy things with*
*my Legos!"*

166

# Jayna's Shadow

My shadow in the morning
Is very very long,
But by the time it's lunchtime
My shadow's almost gone.
It's grown again by dinner.
It's very long and thin.
It gets so big at nighttime.
It lets the stars come in.

*For Jayna, who sent
an e-mail asking for a
poem about shadows.*

167

# Terry Lynn

Terry-Lynn in Flin Flon
Collected lots of rocks,
And hid them in her dresser
In a great big cardboard box.
Her mother wished them long gone
And tried to throw them out
But Terry-Lynn from Flin Flon
Did yell and scream and shout.
She's now collecting boulders.
Her mother says it's wrong.
But Terry-Lynn from Flin Flon
    Keeps collecting on.

*For Terry Lynn Haffich,*
*Flin Flon, Manitoba.*
*"I collect different kinds*
*of neat rocks."*

168

# Neversink School

Our school is near the ocean,
It's really rather neat.
Except that crabs come out at lunch
And nibble at our feet;
And yesterday our teacher
Was eaten by a shark,
Because she stayed late to correct
Our homework after dark.
But we like the ocean
And this is our advice:
"Seaside schools are useful
If your teacher isn't nice."

*For Navesink School,*
*Atlantic Highlands, New Jersey.*

169

# Winter

The great Canadian winter
Is not so very cold.
I once knew a kid who didn't freeze
Until he was ten years old.
And just last year in Ottawa,
When cleaning up the ice,
They found two people still alive
And they said winter was nice.
So don't stay inside when it's snowing,
Don't stay inside when there's ice.
Go out and get frozen like a brick,
And then you'll think winter is nice.

*I wrote this for my own kids
during a cold winter.*

# Chelsea's Dog Spot

My dad does not like Spot.
He wishes he was not.
He wishes we had got
A 'Not Spot' Spot.
But I like Spot a lot.
I don't wish he was not.
I think it would be sad!
If there's a not,
Let's make it Dad!

*For Chelsea Mairs,*
*Ballston Lake, New York.*
*"I have a dog and*
*we named him Spot.*
*My dad does not like Spot."*

# Jeanette Ran Red

Jeanette ran, red to the sunrise,
In the rainbow shining grass;
Rolling in buttercups
And the sweet smell of morning,
Cold dew soaking her nightgown,
Till the inside smell of coffee and pancakes
Rippled through the Queen Anne's Lace.
So rolling and rollicking,
She shivered coldly through the kitchen door
Dropping dew and buttercups and cut grass
Into the warm food smell of kitchen,
And into her mother's surprised "A Springtime Fairy it is,"
Which scooped her up into a very wet
Springtime Hug
Full of worm smell and wet hair.

*For Jeanette, who sent an*
*e-mail wanting a spring poem.*

172

# Goodnight

Goodnight, goodnight, my sleepyhead,
And may your sweet dreams find you,
With jellybeans and chocolate bars
While elves and angels mind you.

*For Andrew and Tyya Munsch,*
*Guelph, Ontario.*

173

# Robert Munsch

**You always tell your stories to kids before making them into books. What happens when you decide that a story is ready to be a book?**

Almost all my books are about real kids, so when a story is ready to become a book, I write to the kid and say, "Send me photos of yourself and your pets and your school and anything else you think will help with the book." So some of the things in my books are done from real photos, and the kid always looks like the real kid I first used in the story. I get together with the artist and we talk about the story and then he does the drawings in pencil and we meet again. Sometimes the story changes in this meeting, because we can do things with the art that I can not do in a "told" story. Then the artist does the whole thing in colour and from then on I can't change any of the story that will change the art. I can still change it in any other way. I keep changing the story as long as I can. Finally, my editor and I have a last meeting where we go over the words and the art for one last time and things *always* change. This is the last time I get to change the story in any way.

**Did you have a playhouse when you were growing up?**

When I was a kid I lived in a very big farmhouse and had five brothers and three sisters. There was a playhouse, and what a playhouse it was! It had two parts with a big roof in between them, so there was lots of room to play, even if it was raining. Under the roof there was a grill for cooking hot dogs, and a sandbox. Now this is the best part: there were two trellises for grapevines and we could climb the trellises and get on the roof. The playhouse was my absolutely favourite place to play. I even liked to be there all by myself, especially if it was raining.

**With so many brothers and sisters, did you have to share a lot when you were a kid?**

We really did share everything. The six boys in the family were all in a row and we shared clothes and food and everything else. I had trouble in school because I shared too much. We were not supposed to share other people's clothes and food. I thought school was a weird place!

**What's the worst haircut you ever had?**

Haircuts were sort of strange when I was a kid. My mom saved money by getting her own hair clippers and cutting all the boys' hair at the same time. But my mom was not a fancy hair clipper! She gave us all a very short buzz-cut so we all looked bald when she was done. This was good for her because it meant that she did not have to cut our hair for a long time. She waited till we were all sort of shaggy and looking like English Sheepdogs, and then she lined us all up and made us bald again. Aaron's long hair reminded me of my long hair, but Aaron's mom never shaved Aaron's head the way my mom shaved mine.

**Is your daughter Julie still crazy about makeup?**

Julie always loved makeup. When she was little, she was always doing face painting on herself or on her little brother, Andrew. Then she went makeup crazy when she was older and discovered lipstick and eye shadow. She spent hours doing makeup! I was sort of hoping that the makeup story would maybe let her get over makeup. It didn't! She is now grown up and she still really, really, really loves makeup.

**Do you still climb trees?**

When I was little I loved to climb. Our yard was excellent for climbing because it had lots and lots of trees. There were small cherry trees with crooked branches that even a two-year-old kid could climb. There were apple and pear and peach trees that were good for six-year-old kids to climb. These were especially good to climb when they were full of apples and peaches and pears! Some days I never ate dinner because of those trees. And there were the very tall and very hard-to-climb maple, oak and tulip trees that were much bigger than the house. I still climb trees even though I am 61 years old. I like to climb really big white pines.

# Michael Martchenko

**What was your first day of school like?**

I remember my first day of school in Canada after my family came here from France. The teacher gave me my own set of crayons, and I didn't have to share them with anyone! I had never had my own crayons before. They also gave us books to write and draw in and every morning they'd give us free milk. I remember I broke one of the crayons one day and I was sure I would get thrown out of school or deported! But no one minded.

**Did you play dress-up when you were a kid?**

I used to pretend a lot with my friends in Brantford. Some days we were cowboys, and others we were soldiers or knights or cavalry men. One time we were paratroopers and we jumped off a really high fence! We would make helmets out of pieces of tubing and paint dragons on cardboard shields. We made swords out of wood and we had bows and arrows that we shot at the garage door. Our garage door looked like a dartboard, it was so full of holes.

We got our ideas from the movies we would go see on weekends. A lot of John Wayne movies. There was only one family in the area that had a television, so a big group of us kids would troop into their house every Saturday morning to watch cartoons and then troop out to go to the theatre and watch movies all afternoon. Plus I would listen to radio shows — cowboys and airplanes and boy stuff like that — while drawing in a school notebook with a pencil.

**Did you climb trees a lot as a kid?**

Actually, we used to climb up the crossbeams in our barn. There was a big pile of grain, and you would cross on these huge rough-hewn beams and jump fifteen feet down into the hay. It was almost like jumping into soft sand, only it would go down your neck and make you itch. As the hay was used for the cattle, the pile would get smaller and smaller and the jump down would be longer and longer.

I also remember climbing fruit trees at my aunt and uncle's fruit farm when I first came to Canada. I was in seventh heaven, surrounded by all the cherries and peaches and pears I could want.

**Did you have a playhouse like Rene's?**

Not exactly. When I lived in Brantford, three friends and I built a shed on the back of one of their houses with scrap wood. It was a glorified lean-to, but we hung out there all the time. We made a door with leather straps for hinges and little lanterns out of jam jars. We lined the inside with cardboard. You couldn't stand up in it, but we used to pretend that it was a cabin at the North Pole.

**Have you ever eaten perogies like Rene's family eats at the end of the story?**

Absolutely! My family is Ukrainian, and my mother used to make mounds and mounds of perogies. We would eat them with fried onions, melted butter and sour cream. My stepfather and I used to have contests to see who could eat the most.

**Where did you get the idea for the courting chickens and other animals in *Playhouse* and other books?**

The ideas just kind of come to me. I think it's funny and the kids think it's funny. You have to make sure the story is visually interesting. We had chicken and pigs and cows at the farm I grew up on.

**What's it like to work with Robert Munsch?**

Bob is a really fun guy, and we work really well together. Sometimes I'll come up with visuals that aren't in the story and Bob and I will work it in together — he lets me run with stuff.

# Alan and Lea Daniel

**What was the worst hair day you ever had?**

*Alan*: I had a pretty terrible haircut when Lea cut my hair for the first time using clippers — she gouged some pretty good hunks out and there was one part that stuck out for about a month.

*Lea*: I once had my hair coloured and then went to a medical appointment where the anaesthetic caused it to turn purple! I had it dyed again, but it took six months for it to look normal.

**Where did the idea come from for the turtle that crawls through the pages of *Aaron's Hair*? Do you have many pets at home?**

*Alan*: It's because of my weird mind — it's a joke, the race between the turtle and the hair. We've had a lot of pets over the years. Just about every pet that you can have, actually! Dogs and cats and worms and guinea pigs. Now we have two granddogs and a grandcat.

*Lea*: We never had a turtle, though.

**Did you go visit Guelph to get ideas for *Aaron's Hair*?**

*Alan*: I had to visit to look at the downtown area and to see the statue, and also to take photos to use as references. I also had to find out what Guelph police uniforms looked like! I did talk to some police officers — one of them looks a lot like one of the policemen in the book. I had to be kind of sneaky about it; I took some photos of the police before going to talk to them.

**Alan, have you ever let your beard grow as long as Aaron's dad's beard in the book?**

*Alan*: Not quite that long, but long enough that kids sometimes confused me with Santa Claus. I had a red jacket and kids in restaurants would point at me. I used to say, "Ho ho ho!" to them, but one little girl was terrified — it turned out she was afraid of Santa Claus.

**Lea, what would you think of a giant beard on Alan?**

*Lea*: No way! But Alan doesn't always remember to trim his beard, so it could happen.

**How did you decide what the characters in the book were going to look like?**

*Alan*: Bob gave us a bunch of pictures, so the the family and the house are based on the real Aaron and his family. I like to include characters from life. It makes it more interesting! The tall skinny guy on the merry-go-round is our son-in-law.

**Who does what when you illustrate together?**

*Lea*: It depends on the book and how much other work we both have.

*Alan*: Lots of times we'll both work on the same page, but it also depends on what technique we're using. In this book, we used different colours of brown coloured pencils for the outlines, and I took it a long way before we started passing it back and forth. I like water-based media like watercolour and gouache. Lea likes acrylics — she keeps sneaking them in! We have different sensibilities and we learn a lot from each other.

**What's the strangest part of working together as a team?**

*Lea*: We have very different schedules. Alan will get up at five or even earlier in the morning and I often work very late.

*Alan*: Sometimes we meet at breakfast. Last night Lea wrote until 5:00 a.m. and I got up at 4:30.